Sticker Dolly Dressing
Fashion Designer
Activity Journal

Designed & illustrated by
Antonia Miller &
Stella Baggott

Written by
Fiona Watt

You'll find the stickers at
the back of the book.

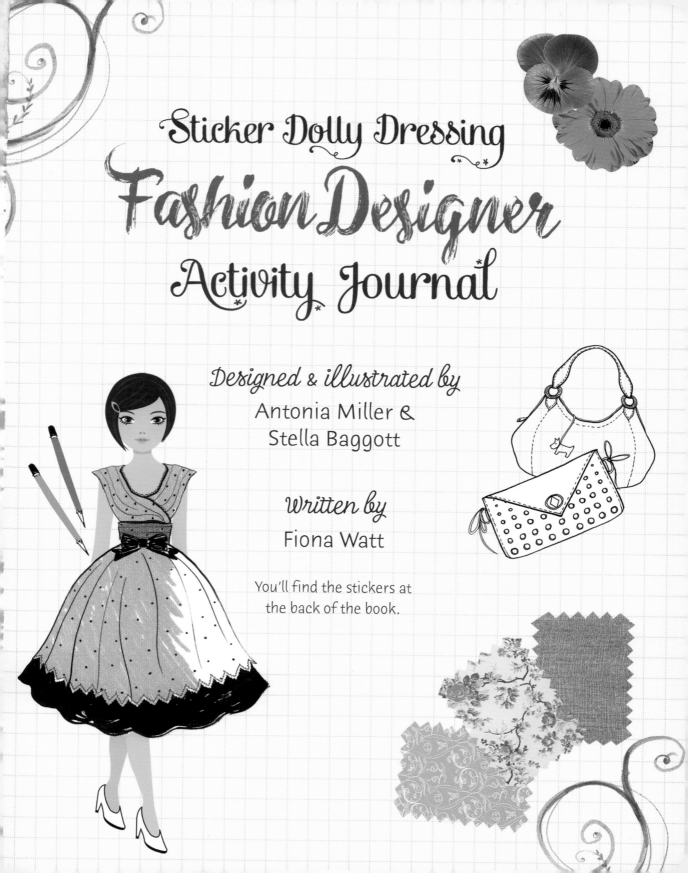

How to use this book

Become a fashion designer by filling the pages with pictures, notes, drawings, designs for materials and color schemes. Here are some ideas of things to do.

Design outfits

Throughout the book there are outlines of dolls for you to draw on. On most of the pages you'll find ideas for what to draw or you could use your imagination and create something entirely of your own.

Tips

Scattered throughout the book there are fashion tips to give you inspiration.

Designer tip:

sketch your idea roughly in pencil before drawing it neatly.

Designer tip:

Use patterned paper from magazines to create clothes.

Coloring in

You'll find line drawings of clothes and accessories such as shoes, bags and jewelry on the backgrounds to color. There are also ideas for different colors to use.

Color the dress, bags and flowers on this page.

Write notes

Label your design with ideas for the types of materials or colors to use.

cardigan - sky blue, knitted?

hot red, deep orange and lilacs

Looking for inspiration

Fashion designers look in lots of different places for inspiration for the styles and colors of their clothes. Look in magazines and newspapers, online and at what people are wearing on television or in the street for ideas.

The natural world

Look at pictures of things in the natural world such as flowers, trees, birds, animals, bugs, the sea, the sky – the list is endless. Study the colors, shapes and patterns.

A skirt inspired by a shell

An evening dress inspired by jellyfish tentacles

Material samples like these are called swatches.

Color the dress, skirt and swatches.

Travel

Look for patterns on buildings, items in markets, the style of the clothes and types of fabrics people are wearing. Take photographs or download pictures of things you spot.

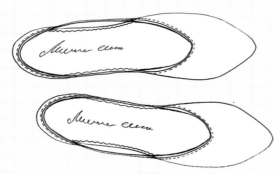

Choose colors and patterns in these photos to fill in the shoes.

Styles from the past

Designers are often inspired by styles of clothes from the past and the fabrics they were made from. Look at old photographs in books and online.

Color this 1960s dress.

Choosing colors

Some colors work well together, while others clash, so it's important to pick your colors carefully.

These colors are known as warm colors.

coral

hot pink

deep pink

magenta

pale yellow

cream

peach

apricot

red

orange

velvet red

maroon

Fill in the clothes with colors from this page.

Cool colors

forest green

purple

spring green

lilac

lime green

turquoise

sky blue

Fill in this outfit
with colors
from this page.

Looking at colors

You could look at pictures for inspiration for
colors to use together.

Fill the circles with some of the
colors you can see in the photos.

Creating a mood board

Fashion designers often create 'mood boards' to show where the inspiration for their clothes, colors and choice of fabrics came from. They make a collage of photos, drawings, samples of fabrics and handwritten notes.

Draw ideas for colors.

Cut out pictures from magazines and glue them on the mood board.

Write notes that describe where your inspiration came from.

Take pictures and stick them in.

Fifties-style dress with full skirt and narrow waist

Design patterns on the stickers from the back of the book.

Add picture stickers to the mood board.

Add samples of actual fabrics.

Stained glass window

Cut out accessories from magazines.

Material from a market in Equador

Include ideas for trimmings and details.

Sketch your ideas.

Color these summer dresses.

Fill the pages with fashion accessories.

Create outfits for spring and summer parties.

spring

Summer

Design casual clothes to
wear on the weekend.

What would be in your dream wardrobe?

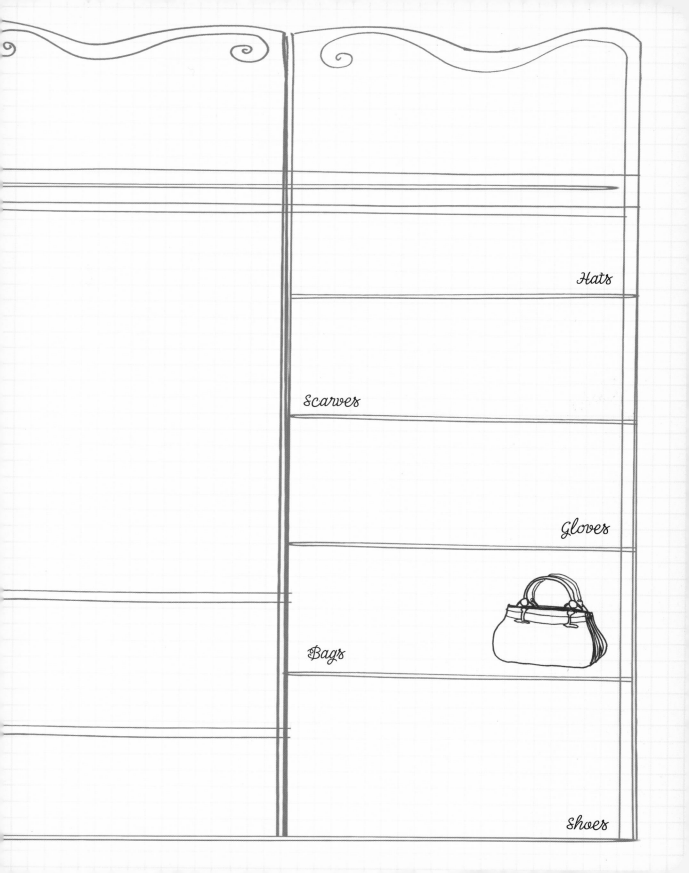

Hats

Scarves

Gloves

Bags

Shoes

Design some necklaces.

Designer tip:

Use a thin pen
for fine details.

styles of skirts

Design outfits with different styles of skirts.

handkerchief

tulip

pleated

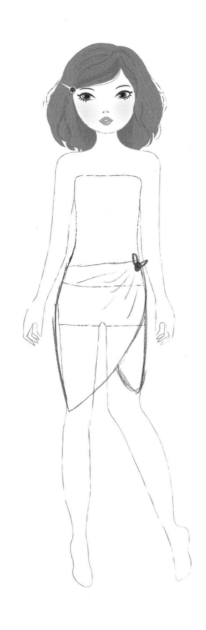

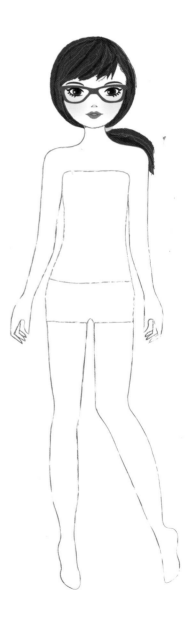

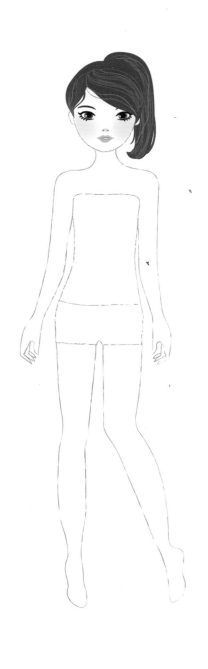

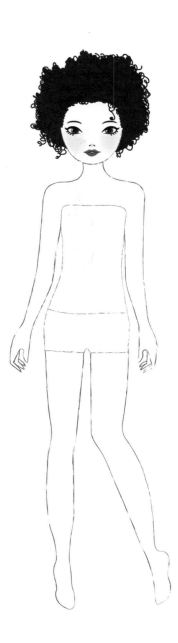

pegged

layered

gathered

Create outfits for a spring collection.

Pastel pinks and
greens

Add springtime colors.

Design dresses for a special night out.

Design patterns on these high-heeled shoes.

lace

animal print

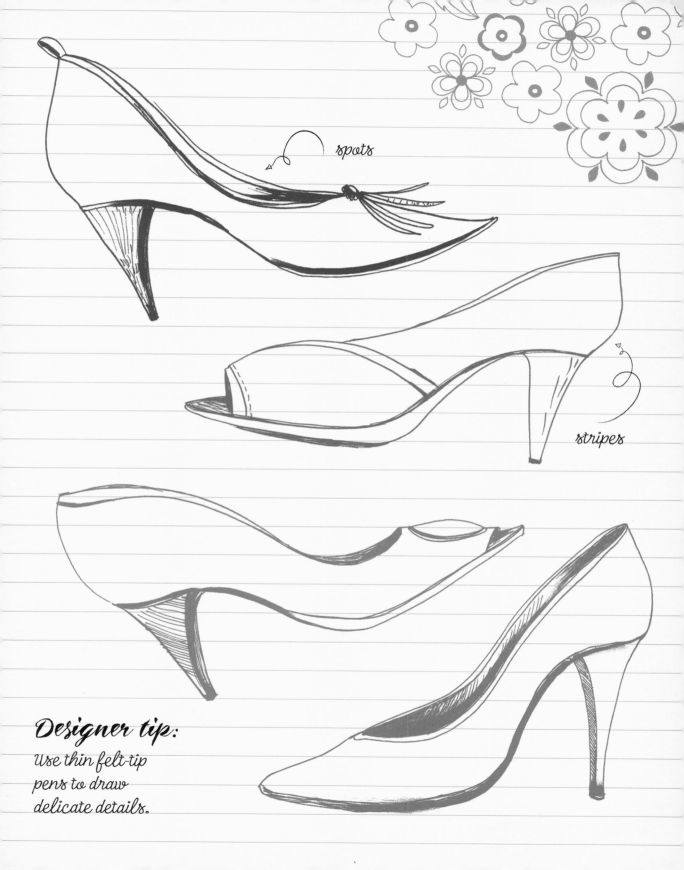

spots

stripes

Designer tip:
Use thin felt-tip
pens to draw
delicate details.

Create mood boards, then design
outfits for the dolls.

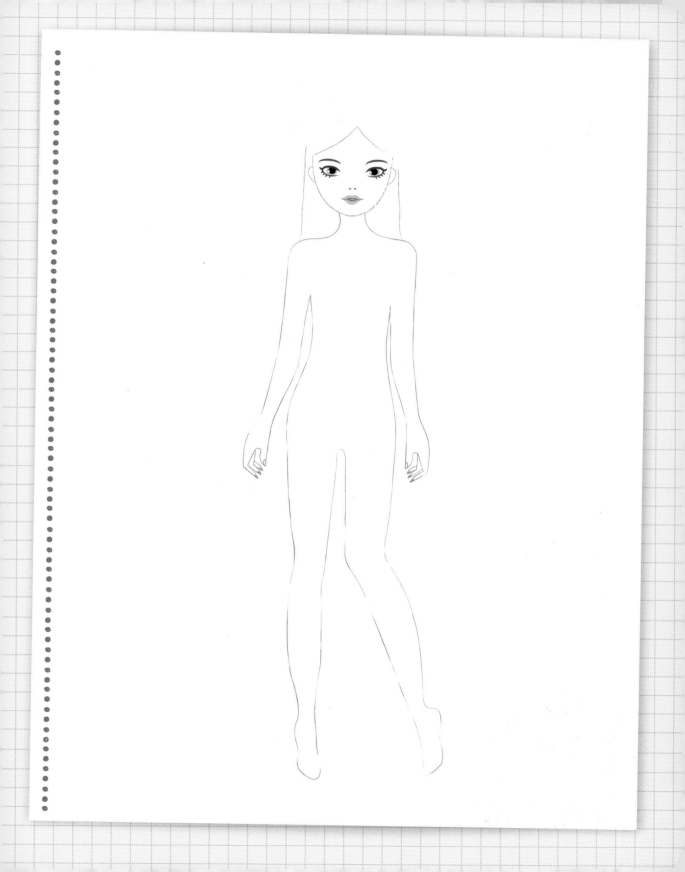

Design and color in the
clothes with red, white
and black patterns.

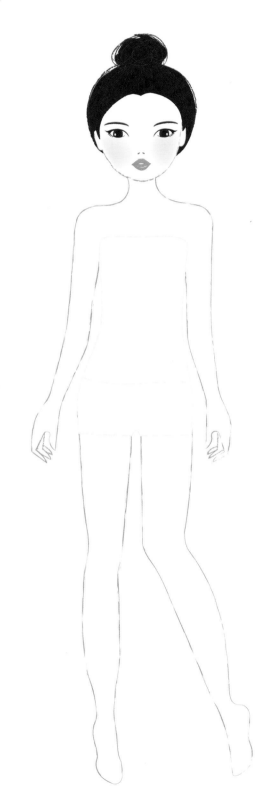

outfits for the catwalk...

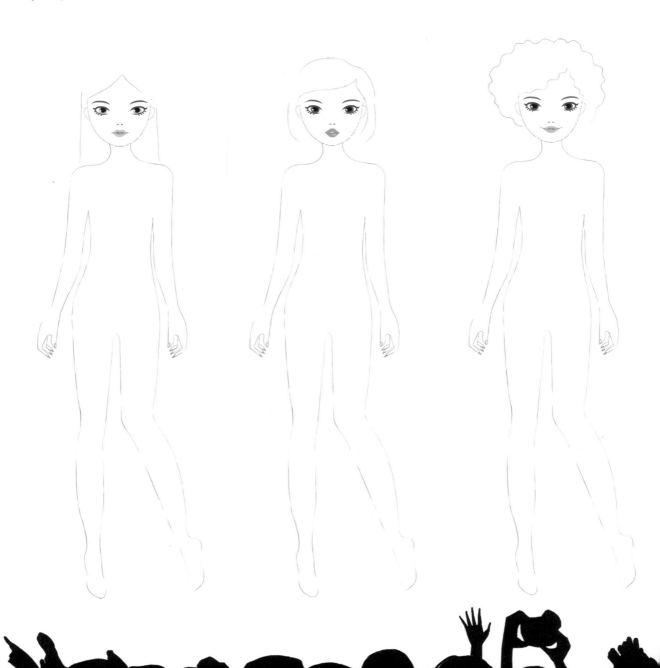

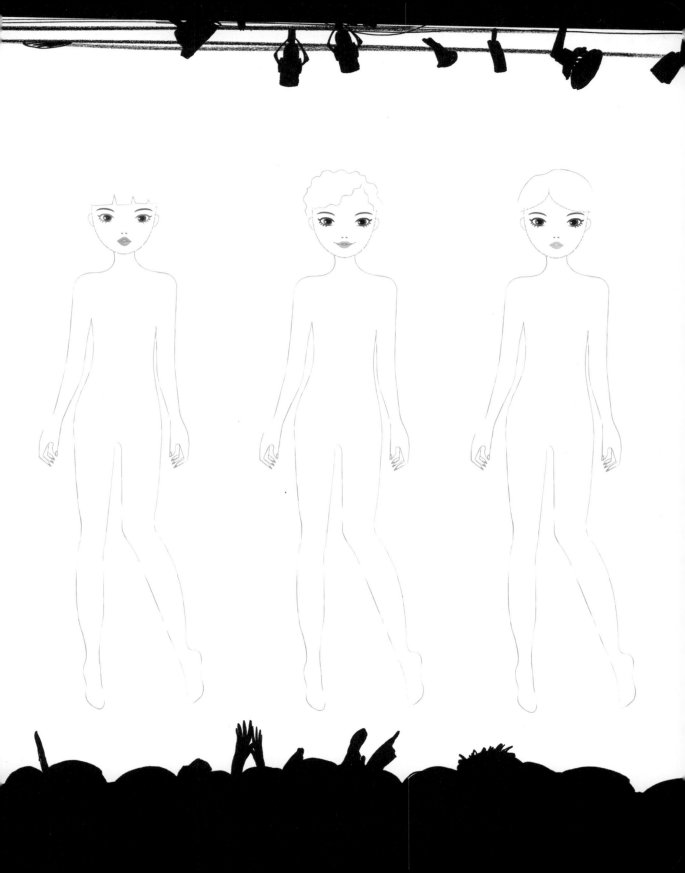

Design prom dresses.

Designer tip:

Draw around the pale shapes for the outlines of the dresses.

Color these patterns, then fill the pages with some of your own.

Designer tip:
Look at patterns on clothes
from around the world.

Design outfits for a summer collection.

Dyed wool from
Marrakech

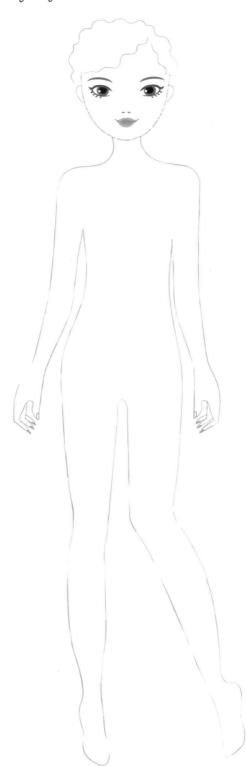

Fresh watermelon
red and green

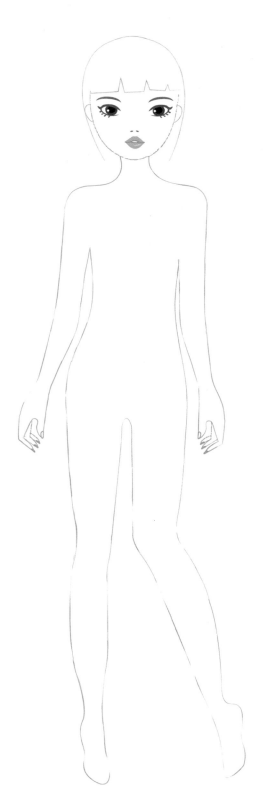

Create mood boards on these pages,
then design outfits from the ideas.

Fill the pages with clothes inspired from fashion around the world.

Japanese kimonos

A Chinese
cheongsam dress

Designer tip:
Look in books
and online for
inspiration.

Create outfits for fall and winter parties.

Fall

Winter

Design outfits with different styles of pants.

straight

skinny

bootleg

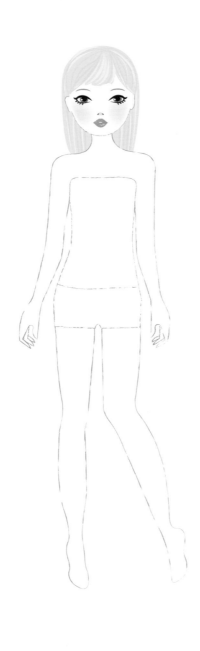

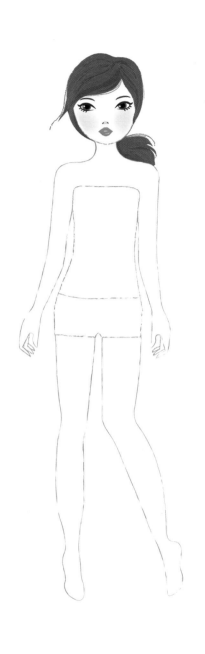

yoga cut out pants

harem

wide leg

cropped

Fill these pages with things that you would take on vacation.

Write a list of things to pack...

Designer tip:

*Think of the type of vacation
it might be before you start.*

Colors of fall
leaves

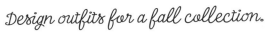
Design outfits for a fall collection.

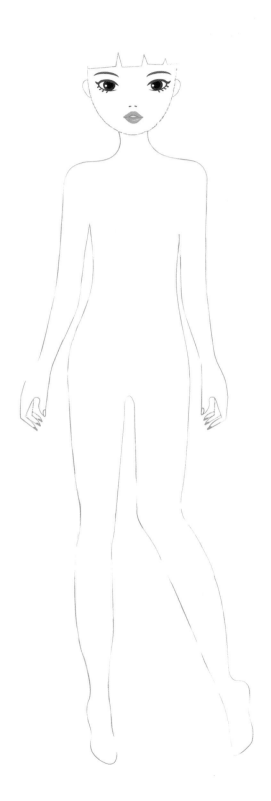

Design swatches of material.

Floral

Folk

Lace

Geometric

Types of patterns: spots, stripes, checkered, animal prints, abstract,

diamonds, polka dots, candy stripes, zigzags, paisley, plaid, gingham...

What would you wear to a costume party?

Create mood boards to show where you found your inspiration, then design outfits for the dolls.

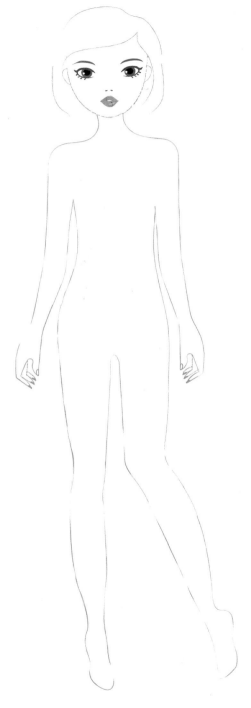

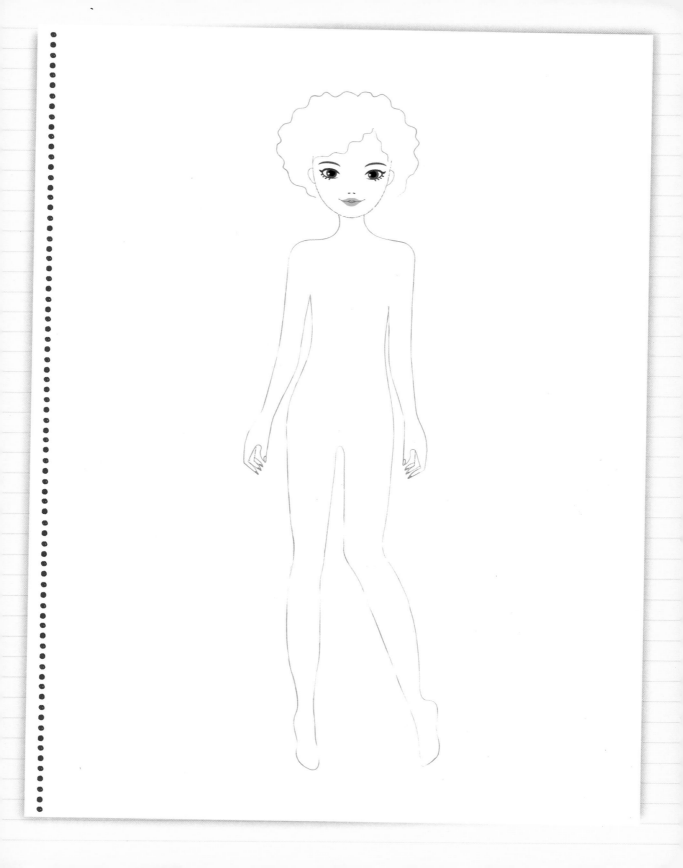

Describe the outfit that you might wear with these ballet flats.

Ideas for colors to use.

Color the shoes.

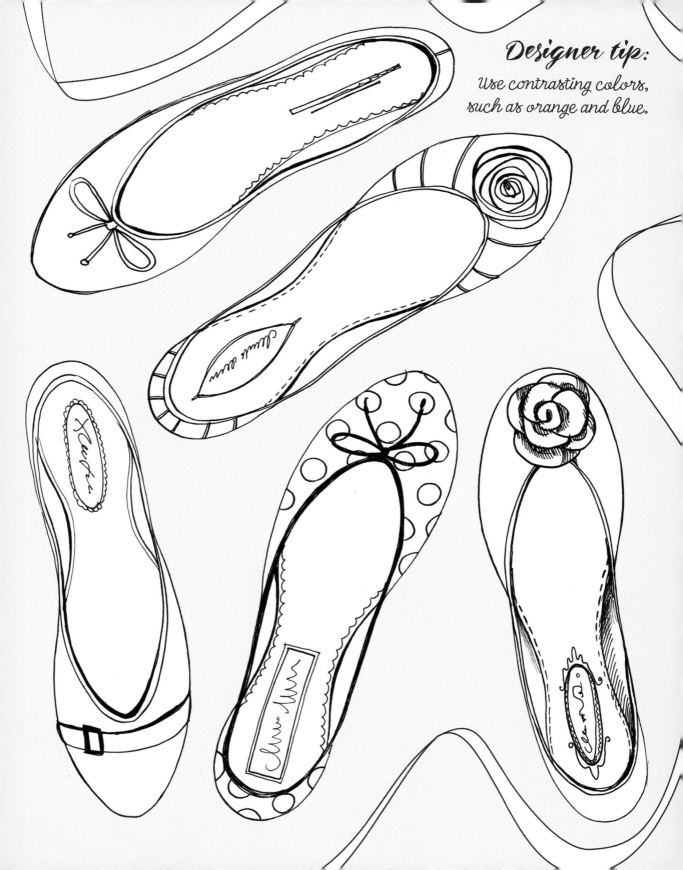

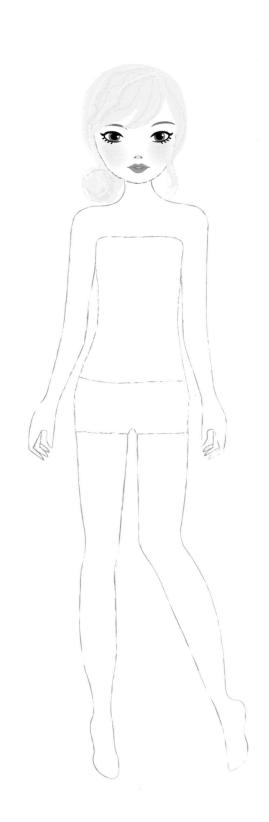

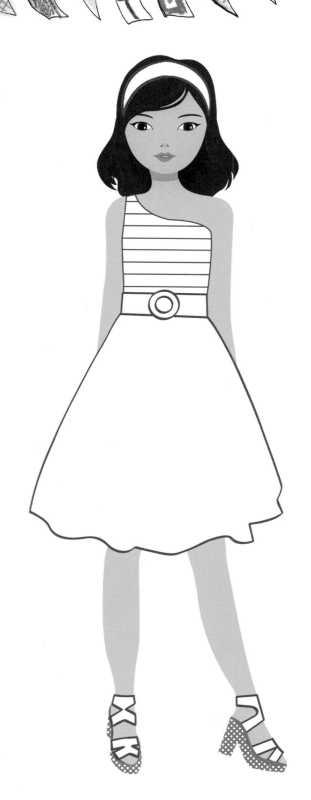

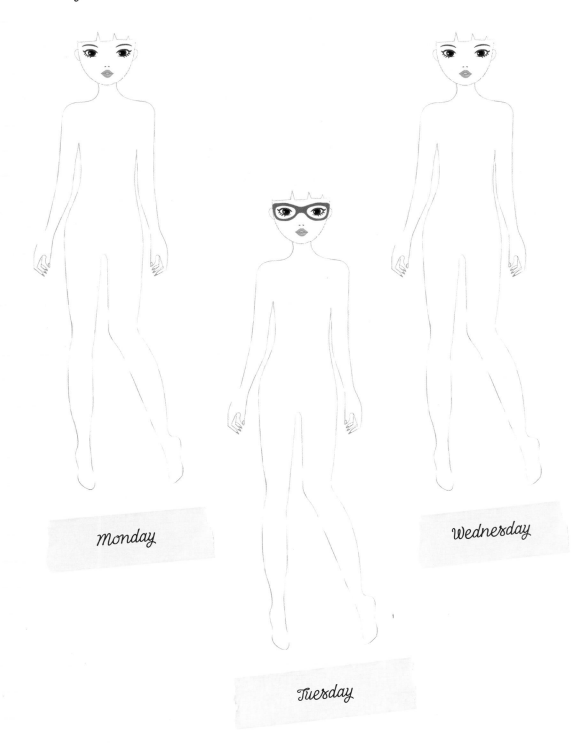

Monday

Tuesday

Wednesday

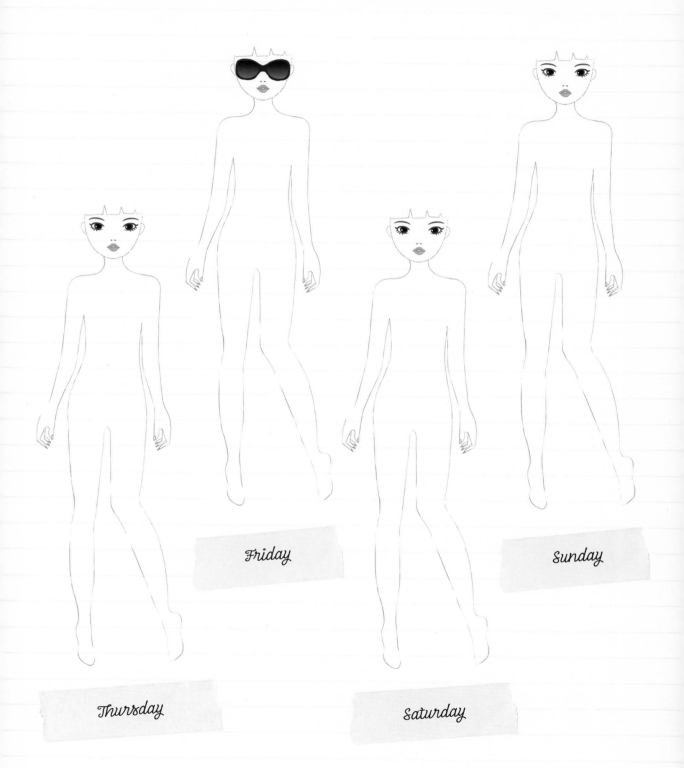

Thursday

Friday

Saturday

Sunday

You could decorate these
wedding dresses with
embroidered patterns,
jewels or lace.

Draw hats for different occasions.

wedding
hat

winter hat

beret

Add more ideas...

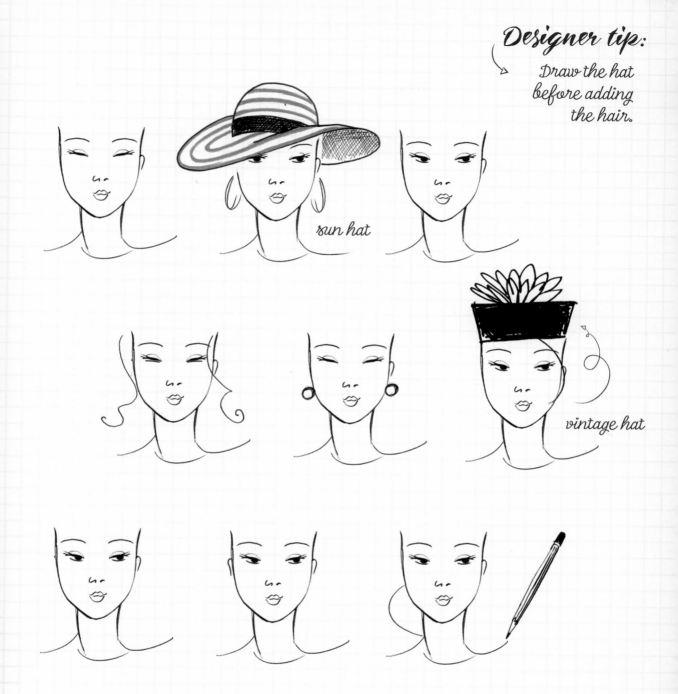

Designer tip: Draw the hat before adding the hair.

sun hat

vintage hat

Create outfits using purples, pinks, black and white.

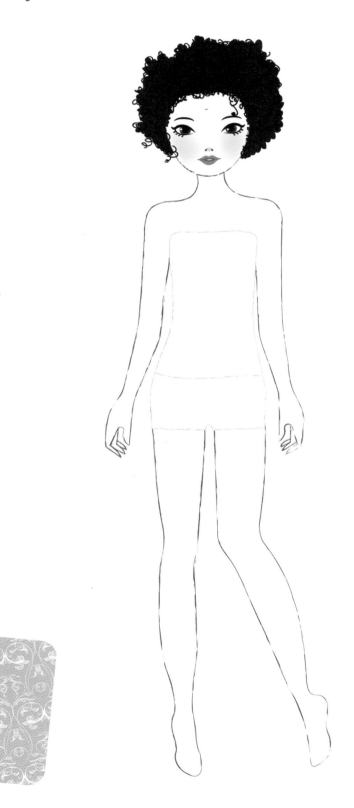

Create mood boards, then design outfits for these dolls.

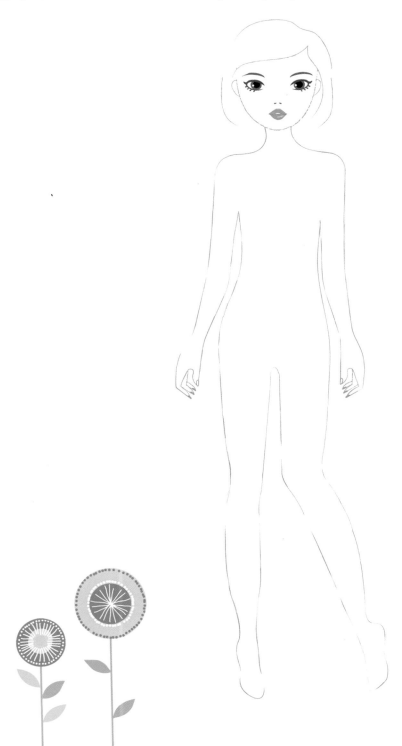

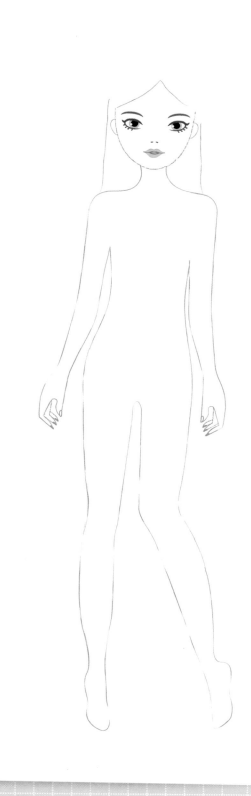

Design styles of shoes, boots and sandals that you'd like...

athletic shoes

high-heeled boots

slingbacks

wedge shoes

ankle boots

basketball high tops

wellington boots

espadrilles

stilettos

party shoes

moccasins

ballet flats

flip flops

classic

vintage

preppy

evening award ceremony

out or dinner date night

Draw your favorite styles.

causanal
arround the
house

out for
the day

sporty

elegant

ethnic

Decorate these skating outfits with sparkly patterns.

You could color these skates to match the outfits.

Design outfits suitable to wear in winter.

Ice blue and white

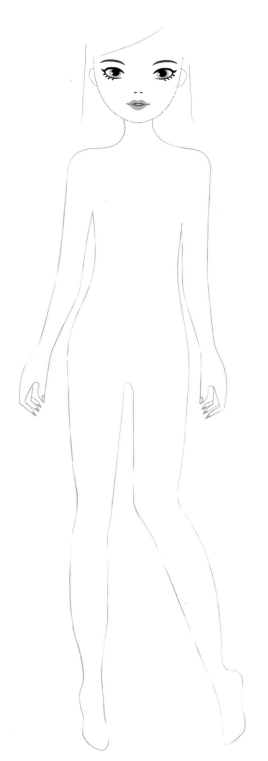

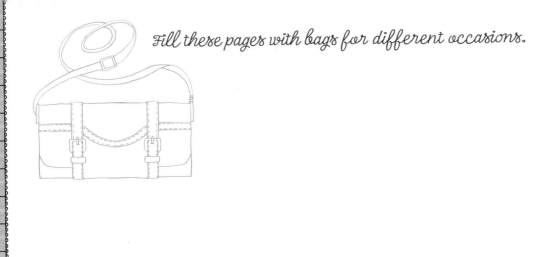

Fill these pages with bags for different occasions.

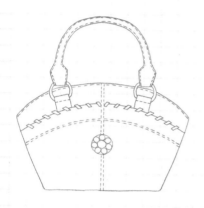

Create outfits inspired by African colors and patterns.

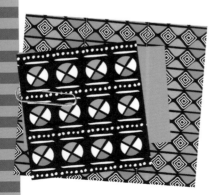

Create outfits with your own choice of colors.

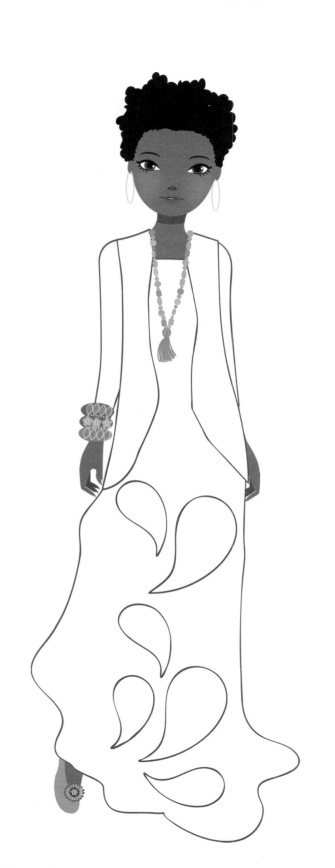

Use the following pages for your own fashion ideas.